The Little Mermaid

Other brilliant stories to collect:

The Little Mermaid

Hans Christian Andersen

Retold by
Linda Newbery

Illustrated by
Bee Willey

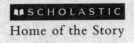
SCHOLASTIC
Home of the Story

Scholastic Children's Books,
Commonwealth House, 1–19 New Oxford Street,
London WC1A 1NU, UK
a division of Scholastic Ltd
London ~ New York ~ Toronto ~ Sydney ~ Auckland
Mexico City ~ New Delhi ~ Hong Kong

First published by Scholastic Ltd, 2001

Text copyright © Linda Newbery, 2001
Illustrations © Bee Willey, 2001

ISBN 0 439 99758 5

Printed by Cox and Wyman Ltd, Reading, Berks.

2 4 6 8 10 9 7 5 3

The right of Linda Newbery and Bee Willey to be identified as the
author and illustrator respectively of this work has been asserted by
them in accordance with the Copyright, Designs and Patents Act, 1988.

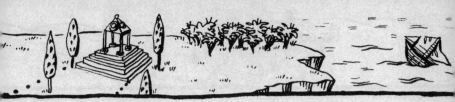

For Arran's class - L.N.

I magine!

Far, far out to sea, the water is bluer than blue, and clearer than the clearest crystal glass. Imagine you can swim there – down, down to the deepest depths, where no human has ever been. Here is a row of little

gardens — each one decorated with shells, and planted with seaweed that waves in the current like hair.

Here, by a marble statue, sits a little mermaid. In her garden, where fish dart in and out like swallows and the water thrums like the song of a harp, the little mermaid is unhappy. She neither sees the fish nor hears the lull of the water-song.

"If only I were fifteen!" she sighs.

She has five older sisters, this mermaid. All are princesses — daughters of the mer-king, whose splendid palace is crusted all over with coral,

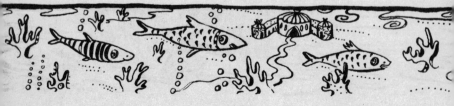

amber and pearls. The mermaid princesses have lost their mother, but otherwise have everything they could possibly want. All except the youngest, the little mermaid.

She longs to see the world of humans above the water.

For this, a mermaid must wait for her fifteenth birthday. Then she may

swim to the surface and sit on a rock, or lie on a sandbank – to see, and to listen. All her sisters have passed fifteen now; each has made her journey, has seen cities and palaces and carriages, and humans walking about on their two legs; and each has decided that the underwater world is best, and is happy to stay there.

But the youngest mermaid looks at her statue, and dreams. It is a statue of a handsome young man. She found it on the sea-bed, lost from a shipwreck, and has planted her garden round it. Sometimes she sings

to it, for she has the most beautiful voice. She gazes at its marble face, and fancies that in the human world above, there will be a living face to match it.

At last, the day of her birthday!

"Goodbye!" she called to her sisters and her grandmother, and she rose through the water on her first journey to the world of humans. Cautiously

she peeped above the surface, not knowing what she would see. It was a calm, still evening, with the sky lit rose-pink. Seeing a splendid three-masted ship, she swam closer. There was barely a breath of wind and the ship was almost still. The little mermaid looked through the cabin windows and saw people and lanterns and tables decked with food.

Her eyes went straight to a beautiful prince, who reminded her of her statue. It seemed to be his birthday; the party was in his honour.

"His birthday, and mine!" she thought.

At midnight, the lanterns were dimmed and the guests went to bed. The waves swelled, rolling the ship to and fro. The wind rushed in, filling the sails; the sky was heavy with clouds. The mermaid, who understood the sea and its weather, knew there would be a fearful storm. To her, a wild sea was a playground – she

dashed and dived through surging waves, and rode high on their crests.

But it was no game for the ship. The sailors heaved on ropes and pulled in sails, but the ship was as frail as a paper boat on a pond. The wind struck again and again, and water rushed over the deck. The timbers

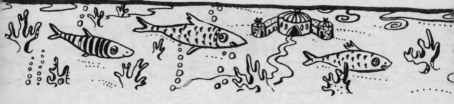

creaked and groaned; and then one mighty blast snapped the main mast and sent the whole ship keeling over.

Now the little mermaid had to look after her own safety, dodging the cracked timbers and the splinters of wreckage. She saw the young prince flung into the water, swimming, and sinking – at first she was delighted, for now he would come to live underwater. But then she remembered that human beings cannot survive in water – only if the prince were dead could he visit her father's palace.

No! He mustn't die!

She dived deep, and caught him as he sank, pulled down by the current. His eyes were closed, his limbs already numb. She swam hard, pushing up to the surface with all the muscular strength of her tail. All through the night, the little mermaid held him, supporting him till her arms and tail ached with weariness.

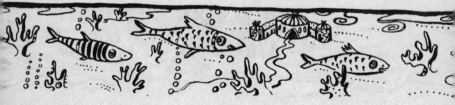

Dawn came, and the first light lit the prince's face. She kissed him and prayed that he would live. She sang to him, just as she sang to her statue. She swam, not knowing where to take him.

At last she saw land – snow-clad mountains, green forests, and a holy temple. She carried her prince to the bay, and laid him to rest on the sand. Soon, people came from the temple. A dark-haired girl called out and ran to the shore, and suddenly there was a great commotion – one person tipped the prince face-down, another slapped his cheeks, the young girl rubbed his

hands. The mermaid, hiding behind rocks, watched and watched – and at last he coughed and spluttered, and sat up. He was alive! There were exclamations of joy and relief. The prince, gaining strength, smiled at the young girl who held his hand, and spoke to the people around him; they wrapped him in a cloak, and led him away.

The little mermaid was glad that he was alive — but sad that he had smiled at all those people but never once at her, for he did not know who his real rescuer was.

She returned to the mer-king's palace, silent and thoughtful.

"Well?" her sisters asked her. "Where did you go? What did you see? What did you do?"

But the little mermaid went to sit in her garden by herself. Mermaids cannot shed tears, or she would have wept.

Many a time, in the following days,

she swam to the shore by the temple. She saw people come and go, heard their chatter, but never once did she see her handsome prince.

At last she could bear it no longer. She whispered her secret to one of her sisters.

"I know who you mean! I can show you where his palace is!" said the sister. The magnificent palace faced the

seashore. It was built of glistening stone, with great flights of marble steps. There were statues, fountains, domes. There was a garden, whose flowers and greenery looked to the little mermaid far superior to the straggles of weed in her own garden.

Day by day she grew fascinated by the world of humans. She would rise from the water and gaze at the palace, longing for a glimpse of her love. Growing braver, she swam up the river inlet, next to the marble terrace. Often she saw him – strolling in the garden, or sailing, or talking to friends.

One evening, she swam back and sought out her wise grandmother.

"If humans don't drown," she asked, "do they live for ever? Or do they die as we do, after three hundred years?"

"Oh yes, they die," said the grandmother, "and their lives are much shorter than ours. But when we die, we turn into foam on the sea, and

that's the end of us. Humans have immortal souls – their souls live for ever, among the stars, in places we can only dream of!"

"Why can't we have immortal souls?" asked the little mermaid. "I'd give anything to be human! I'd give up some of my three hundred years if I could live for ever in that place in the stars!"

"Don't talk like that, silly girl!" the grandmother chided. "We're much better off down here." And she called an angel fish to her, and fed it from her hand.

"Is there no way I can get an immortal soul?" persisted the little mermaid.

"There's only one way," said the grandmother. "If you can get a human man to love you, to wish more than anything to marry you, to be bound to you for all eternity – then he'll give you an immortal soul, while keeping his own." Then she laughed, and

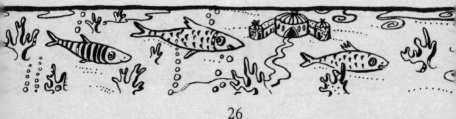

pointed to their tails. "But how can
that happen? Our tails, our greatest
beauty, are thought by humans to be
monstrous. For them to find you pret-
ty, you need two of those stumpy
things they call legs."

"Oh," said the mermaid, looking
down at her green scaly tail.

"Cheer up!" said the grandmother.
"There's a ball tonight, and you're to
sing. We know how to enjoy ourselves,
in our three hundred years."

That evening the princess sang and
everyone admired her voice, which
was far more beautiful than the voice

of any human. The palace was flooded with light, and all kinds of fish, great and small, colourful as fragments from a kaleidoscope, came to watch the festivities.

Everyone danced and laughed and ate – everyone but the little mermaid, who only wanted to dream of her prince in the world above. She left the palace to sit alone in her garden.

I love him, yet he doesn't know I exist, she thought. I'd give anything to be with him!

She knew of only one person who might help her – the sea-witch, of whom everyone was afraid. But the little mermaid was ready to risk anything to win the love of her prince.

While it was still dark, the little mermaid ventured across deserts of sand and through roaring whirlpools. Beyond, the sea-witch lived in a cave in the midst of a weird forest. The trees and bushes were half-human, half-animal – they stretched and

leered at the little mermaid. She hesitated, afraid to pass through. Some clasped bones of drowned fishermen in their tentacles; others reached out their slimy arms to grab her. She almost lost heart and turned back; then she thought of her prince, closed her eyes and darted, slick as quicksilver, past the monstrous trees to the cave beyond.

There sat the sea-witch, with water-snakes crawling all over her and in and out of her hair.

"I know why you've come!" she said straight away. "And you shall have it, for it will lead you into trouble. You want to exchange your fish's tail for two ugly stumps, like humans have. You want that prince to fall in love with you, and give you an immortal soul. Yes?"

"Yes," confessed the mermaid.

The sea-witch laughed so loudly that all the snakes fell out of her hair and wriggled about on the slimy sea-bed.

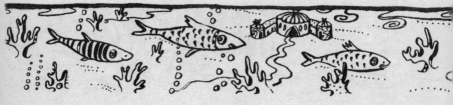

"I'll make you a potion," she said, "and you must swim to a sand-bank near this prince's palace, then drink it up. Your tail will shrivel up and divide into two stumps, that men call legs, and then you'll be able to walk on land. But it will hurt! It will feel like a sharp sword slicing through you. And every step you take will feel like walking on knives. Are you stupid enough to do all that, for this man you hardly know?"

"Yes," said the mermaid, trembling.

The witch laughed nastily. "Yes, I thought so. Remember, you'll never

be a mermaid again – you'll never see your sisters, or your grandmother, or your father's palace. And if the prince doesn't love you more than anyone else, you won't get an immortal soul! If he marries someone else, your heart will break, and the very next morning you'll turn into foam of the sea. Still want to do it?"

"Yes," said the mermaid, shivering.

"Then," said the witch, "you must pay me. Your voice is more beautiful than anyone's – I'm having that, for my wages. You're not going to charm him that way!"

"But with no voice," said the little mermaid, "what have I left?"

"Your lovely face," sneered the witch. "Your beautiful shape. Your speaking eyes. That's enough, isn't it, to bewitch a mere man? Oh, having second thoughts, are you? Not such a good idea, now?"

"I'll do it!" said the little mermaid, on a surge of defiance.

The witch laughed and scoured her cauldron with a handful of snakes. Then she slit her little finger and let the black blood drip into the pot. She threw in more ingredients — sea-slugs, rotting weed, toad-slime. Foul-smelling steam rose from the cauldron and took the shape of grinning faces. At last the potion was brewed and the liquid turned clear.

"All done!" said the witch, sniffing it. She poured some into a glass vial. "Now, my price."

And she pointed a knobbly finger at the little mermaid's mouth. At once, the mermaid's tongue burned and shrivelled to nothing. She tried to speak, but could not make a sound.

"Now go away," said the witch, settling down for a rest with her snakes and toads.

The little mermaid swam quickly back to her father's palace, clutching the vial. The palace was still in darkness and everyone still asleep. The little

mermaid dared not go in; instead, she swam through all her sisters' gardens, plucking one flower from each. Mermaids cannot shed tears, or she would have wept.

The sun had not yet risen when she reached the shore facing the prince's palace. She swam to the marble steps, and there she drank the potion.

It burned and stung her poor shrivelled tongue and her throat; and at once she felt the sharpest, most unbearable pain slicing through her. She gave a soundless scream and fainted.

She woke to daylight and a fresh stab of pain; and then she saw that her prince had come! His coal-black eyes were looking at her, tender and anxious. She looked down and saw that she had a pair of slender legs instead of her tail; but she was naked, so she wrapped her long hair around her body.

"Who are you? Where have you come from?" the prince asked, kneeling.

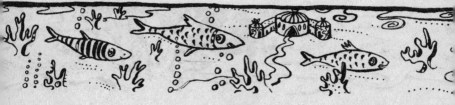

She could not tell him; she looked at him yearningly. He took her hand and helped her up. She took her first steps on human feet – and each step, just as the sea-witch had said, was like treading on sharp knives. But she would not let the pain show in her face; she clutched her hair around her and smiled gratefully.

Everyone in the palace marvelled at her beauty. She was given fine clothes, and good things to eat; but she was dumb, and could not thank them.

There were parties, and the little mermaid wished so desperately that she could sing to her prince, to tell him of her love. She could only applaud other singers whose voices sounded cracked and strained, compared to the memory of her own water-music.

Instead, she danced for him. She was the most graceful dancer in the palace, even though with each twirling step,

each pirouette, she felt the stab of a hundred razor-sharp daggers. When the dancing was over, and everyone in bed, she went outside to paddle in the sea, letting the water cool her burning feet. And she fancied that in the shimmer of moonlight on water she saw her mermaid sisters, raising their heads to call to her and stretching out their arms.

She became the prince's favourite companion, and spent every day and evening with him. He loved her; but not as she wanted to be loved.

"There's only one girl I'll ever marry," he told her as they sat together one evening. "You remind me of her – the girl who rescued me!"

The little mermaid gazed at him, her eyes imploring. Had he opened his eyes after all, while he was lifeless in the water – had he seen her?

"But I'll never win her love," the prince said sadly. "She belongs to the holy temple. She lives a life of prayer

and contemplation. What use has she for husband, marriage or home? Yet I owe her my life! I would have drowned had she not pulled me from the sea!"

No! No! The little mermaid tried to tell him. *I* was the one who saved you, who pulled you from the deeps and used all my strength to support you!

"I shall never forget that beautiful

face!" said the prince, half to himself; then he turned to the mermaid. "You understand, don't you? There is a sadness about you. You understand what it is to long for something with your heart and soul and to be denied it?"

Oh yes, she understood!

"And now I'm to visit the king of the next country," the prince grumbled. "They expect me to marry his daughter, but I shan't! I'll marry no one but my girl of the temple. You'll come with me, won't you my dearest friend, to while away the tedium?"

The prince's new ship set sail, and the prince stood on deck with the little mermaid, telling her of the wonders of the deep: the strange creatures, the dark caverns, the marvels that even divers had not seen. She smiled to hear him talk, for she knew much better than he! And she longed for the visit to be over, and to have her

beloved prince to herself again, for she knew he had no interest in the foreign king's daughter.

When the prince's ship docked in the harbour of the magnificent city, there were parties, and processions, and parades, and the prince was always the guest of honour – but of the king's daughter there was no sign.

"She will be here soon," the little mermaid heard one of the court attendants say, "when she comes back from her studies at the holy temple. And then there will be a wedding, for this prince cannot help but fall in love

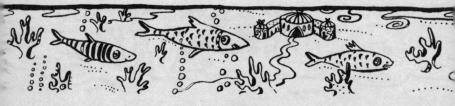

with her. What a fine pair they will make! For she is his match in beauty, grace and wealth."

At the words "holy temple", the little mermaid shivered, for she knew now who the king's daughter was, and that the prince loved her already. The young girl came home two days later and shyly greeted her future husband. When the little mermaid saw the lovely face, the long dark hair and shining eyes, she felt a cold tremor pass through her. She would never win the prince's love now, for he was overjoyed to find himself paired with his true

love, the girl from the holy temple, the girl he believed had saved him.

"You're happy for me, aren't you, my dear friend?" the prince asked the little mermaid, the night before the wedding. "I am happier than I ever dreamed! But you will always be my friend – and hers! For she must love you as well as I do."

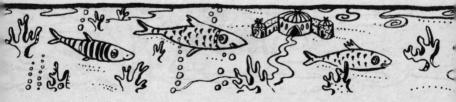

The wedding was a splendid
occasion. Bells pealed and heralds
trumpeted, and the church was decked
with flowers. The bride and groom,
gorgeously dressed, held hands and
were blessed by the bishop, and pro-
claimed husband and wife. The little
mermaid, dressed in silk and gold,
held the bride's train. But she heard
and saw little of the ceremony – she
could think only of her coming death,
and of all that she had gained, and lost.

The wedding party that night was
held on board the prince's ship. When
the dancing began, the little mermaid

remembered the first night she had danced for her prince. She would dance again, for the very last time! And she threw herself into the music, skimming, twirling, whirling, and everyone stopped dancing to cheer her. Each step sent pain searing through her feet, yet she hardly noticed, for the pain in her heart was so much sharper.

At last the prince and his bride went to their royal bed and the little mermaid stood alone on the deck, gazing out to sea. She would die with the first rays of dawn light. She would never see her beloved prince again, nor have an immortal soul.

Out on the bobbing waves, she saw the glimmer of pale faces, and arms stretched towards her. Her sisters! But she stared – how strange they looked! Their long hair had gone, sheared to stubble!

"Sister!" they called. "We've given our hair to the sea-witch, to make her

help us! Do what we tell you!" The mermaid saw the flash of moonlight on steel. "Take this knife! Before the sun rises, you must plunge it into the prince's heart! When his blood sprinkles your feet, they'll disappear and turn back into your mermaid's tail, and you'll be able to come home with us and live out your three hundred years! But hurry! Can't you see how the sky is lightening?"

The little mermaid reached down for the knife and her sisters sank beneath the water.

With heavy heart, she crept into

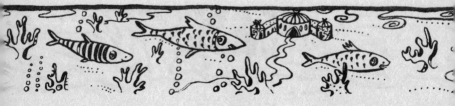

the prince's bedroom. There he slept,
with his lovely bride cradled close; the
little mermaid kissed him and then he
murmured the name of his bride, his
beloved. He had no thought for
anyone but her!

The little mermaid raised the knife
– how heavy it was, and how sharp! –

and held it poised. She thought of all
the cutting pain she had endured for
his sake.

Then, making her choice, she
lowered it. She ran to the deck, and
with all her strength hurled the dagger
into the waves. For a second it hung
in the air, catching the first rosy
dawn light.

Her eyes already dimming, she threw herself overboard and her body dissolved into foam of the sea.

Now the sun rose, and its kindly beams warmed the foam, so that the little mermaid did not feel the chill of death. Instead, she saw the sun, and the air above, filled with wispy shapes and silvery voices.

"Where am I going?" she asked.

A voice replied, "You are with the Daughters of the Air! You, poor little mermaid, had no immortal soul, but you have yearned for something with your whole heart, and now you are rewarded

for your good deeds! Come with us!"

And the little mermaid saw that she had a new shape, a wispy, transparent shape like theirs, risen out of the foam. Together they floated, light as bubbles, laughing.

She gazed down at the ship, and thought of her prince lying there asleep, his arms entwined with his

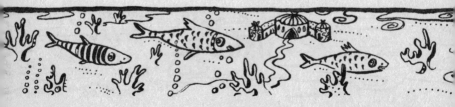

bride's. She felt sad for him; he would never know where she had gone, or what she had done for him.

"Come, sister! Fly higher!" urged the silvery voice. "For our spirit world is more beautiful than you can ever imagine."

The little mermaid looked up into the golden, streaming light, and at her new sisters, the Daughters of the Air. Then she looked down towards her prince for the last time. She must leave him now.

"Goodbye," she whispered; and for the first time she shed tears.

Other stories to collect:

The Ugly Duckling

Helen Dunmore

Illustrated by Robin Bell Corfield

Once upon a time there was an ugly duckling
that didn't have a friend in the world...

Orpheus in the
Land of the Dead

Dennis Hamley

Illustrated by Stuart Robertson

Once upon a time there was a musician so fine
that even the dead were charmed...

The Musicians of Bremen

Ann Jungman

Illustrated by James Marsh

Once upon a time there was a donkey
who ran away from home…

Beauty and the Beast

Tessa Krailing

Illustrated by Diana Mayo

Once upon a time there was a beautiful girl
who was forced to live with a hideous Beast…

King Herla's Ride

Jan Mark

Illustrated by Jac Jones

Once upon a time there was a king who lived
upon a hill and a king who lived under one…

The Pedlar of
Swaffham

Philippa Pearce

Illustrated by Rosamund Fowler

Once upon a time there was a pedlar
who had an unforgettable dream…

Hansel and Gretel

Henrietta Branford

Illustrated by Lesley Harker

Once upon a time there were a brother and sister
who were left alone in the forest…

Mossycoat

Philip Pullman

Illustrated by Peter Bailey

Once upon a time there was a beautiful girl
whose mother made her a magical, mossy coat…

Aesop's Fables

Malorie Blackman

Illustrated by Patrice Aggs

Once upon a time there was a man named Aesop
who told stories full of wisdom...

The Snow Queen

Berlie Doherty

Illustrated by Sian Bailey

Once upon a time there was a little boy
whose heart was turned to ice...